To: Lincolwood Library

Thank you so much for having me!

Bless up!

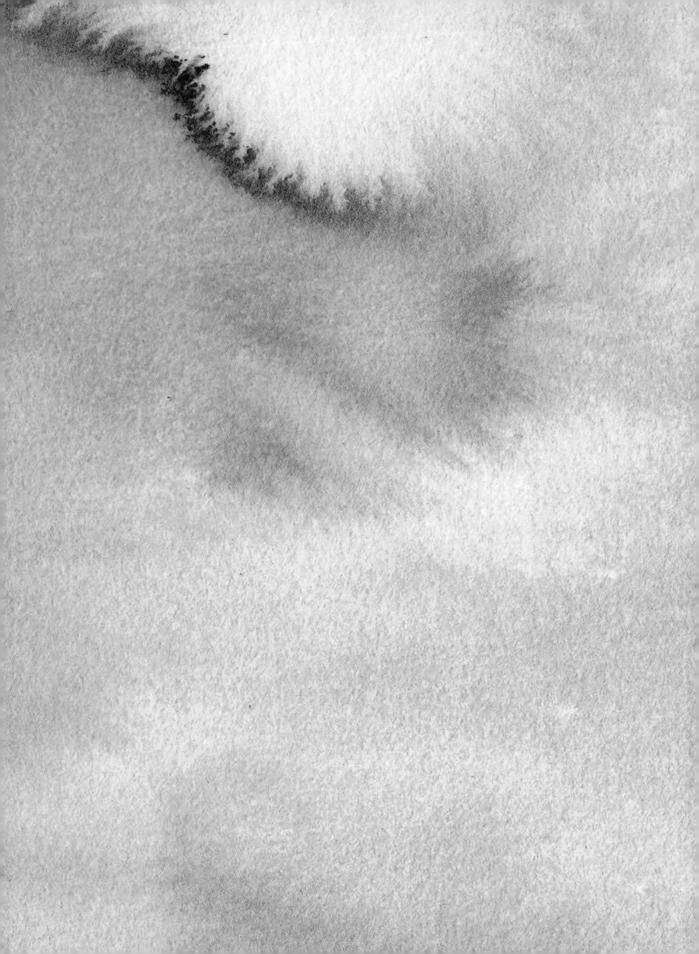

This book is dedicated to my family and friends, and all who have left their homes in search of something better.

www.mascotbooks.com

Amoya's Big Move

For more information, please contact:
Mascot Books
620 Herndon Parkway, Suite 320
Herndon, VA 20170
info@mascotbooks.com

Library of Congress Control Number: 2017918865

CPSIA Code: PRT0418A
ISBN-13: 978-1-68401-390-6

Printed in the United States

AMOYA'S BIG MOVE

Written by
DAHLIA RICHARDS

Illustrated by
TERRI KELLEHER

"Wake up, Moya! The sun is shining and today's the big day!"

That's my mommy, Angela. She's excited because we're moving to Chicago today to live with her parents. I wish I was as excited, but I'm not.

As soon as Mommy leaves, I cover my face with the sheet to block the sun. But it's no use. The glass slats in the window don't help much either.

Slowly, I roll out of bed and look for my slippers. "Yuh will ketch cold!" I can already hear my mommy's warning if I dare to walk out of my room without something on my feet.

My sister's bed is made and everything is in its place. Why make the bed if we're leaving today anyway?

"¡Despiértate, Moya! ¡El sol está brillando y hoy es nuestro día!"

Es mi Mamá, Ángela. Ella está emocionada porque hoy nos vamos a vivir a Chicago con sus padres. Quiero estar tan emocionada como ella, pero no lo estoy.

Cuando se va, meto la cara debajo de las sábanas para esconderme del sol. Pero no sirve de nada. Los listones de vidrio de la ventana tampoco ayudan.

Despacito, me levanto de la cama y busco mis chanclas. " ¡Te vas a morir de la gripa!" Es lo que dirá mi mamá si salgo de mi cuarto sin algo en lo pies.

La cama de mi hermana está hecha y todo está en su lugar. ¿Y para qué hacer la cama si de todas maneras nos vamos hoy?

In the kitchen, my sister Denise is already mixing the Horlicks tea. *Mmm!* My favorite!

"The fried dumpling inna the pudding pan behind you," Denise says.

I spin around, grab two of them, and head to the veranda to eat. I sit on a suitcase and put the two hot dumplings in my lap so I can watch as everyone walks up the hill to say their goodbyes.

Suddenly, my brother runs past and grabs one of my dumplings.

"MOMMY!!!" I yell. "The ole big head boy just thief mi breakfast!"

Mommy pokes her head out of her window. "Hurry up and finish so mi cyaa comb yuh hair."

En la cocina, mi hermana Denise ya está mezclando el té de Horlicks. Mmm! Mi favorito!

"Los dumplings (bolas de masa) están atrás de ti," dice Denise. Me doy la vuelta, agarro dos dumplings y camino hacia el porche para comérmelos. Me siento en la maleta y pongo los dumplings en mis piernas.

De repente, mi hermano aparece corriendo muy rápido y me roba una.

"¡MAMAAA!" grito. "!El niño cabezón me robo mi desayuno!"

Ella saca la cabeza por la ventana y dice, "Date prisa y come. Tengo que peinarte el cabello."

I take a big bite of my last dumpling and a big slurp of my tea.

"Amoya, yuh have to drink the tea like that?" Denise asks me, handing me another dumpling.

"If I don't want it to burn off my mouth," I answer her. Denise hates when I slurp my tea. I make another big slurp as she sits down next to me.

"This morning, Jamaica. Tonight, Chicago," she says.

By the time my hair is combed, the whole family is there.

"Leave Amoya's uniform for Nadine. They don't wear uniform like that in foreign," says Aunt Claudia.

"Leave the bedspread for me, Angela," calls someone else. Anything that's staying behind will go to the family.

"My cleats are coming with me!" my brother yells out. I guess he plans to play football in the snow!

Tomo un mordisco grande de mi último dumpling y un gran sorbo de mi te.

"¿Amoya, tienes que beber así?" Denise me pregunta, dándome otro dumpling.

"Si, no quiero quemarme la boca," yo respondo. Ella odia ese ruido.

Hago otro gran sorbo mientras ella se sienta a mi lado.

"Por la mañana, Jamaica. Por la noche, Chicago," dice ella.

Cuando mi mama termina de peinarme llega toda la familia.

"Deja el uniforme de Amoya para Nadine. Allí no se los ponen," dice tía Claudia.

"Deja esas sábanas para mi, Ángela," dice alguien más. Todo lo que no nos llevemos se va a quedar con nuestra familia.

"¡No voy a dejar mis zapatos de fútbol" grita mi hermano. ¡Quizá él piensa que va a jugar fútbol en la nieve!

I grab my cousin Nadine's hand and pull her to my room so I can finish getting dressed.

"Promise you'll write me," she says as we hug each other tight.

"Of course I'll write you! I'll make Mommy send you a big dolly too! One with tall, tall hair and jeans pants."

We lay on my bed and I'm very careful not to mess up my hair. Not too long after, I hear the sound of the van coming down the street.

"Amoya, Denise, Ryan! Grab yuh suitcase and mek your cousin help yuh carry them down to the van," Mommy yells.

My eyes immediately fill up with water. I blink a few times until it goes away.

Agarro la mano de mi prima Nadine y caminamos hacia mi cuarto para terminar de vestirme.

"Prométeme que me vas a escribir," me dice ella y nos abrazamos fuerte.

"¡Claro que sí! ¡Y también, voy a convencer a mi mamá para que te mande una muñeca grande, con el pelo bien largo y con pantalones!"

Nos acostamos con cuidado en mi cama para no estropear mi pelo. Un poco después, escucho la camioneta.

"¡Amoya, Denise, Ryan! Tomen sus maletas y díganle a sus primos que les ayuden a llevarlas a la camioneta," grita Mamá.

De repente, se me aguan los ojos, pero los parpadeo varias veces hasta que se me secan.

"Grab the other side, Moya. I'll help you with this one," Nadine says.

We struggle to carry the suitcase to the veranda. Ryan must have superhuman strength because he grabs both of our suitcases and starts down the hill.

"Well excuse me, Superman," I call. Farther down the hill, his little girlfriend is waiting for him. I should've known he was showing off for a reason.

"Amoya agarra por este lado y yo te ayudo por el otro," dice Nadine.

Nos costó llevar la maleta al porche. Ryan, por supuesto, tiene fuerza súper humana porque agarra su maleta y la mía y empieza a bajar la colina.

"¡Perdón, Superman!" grito. Al final de la colina, veo a su novia. Debería haber sabido que lo hacía para presumir.

Soon, the back of the van is spilling over with suitcases. "Can I sit in the back with Ryan and Denise?" I ask Mommy.

"Mek sure yuh put her where she won't fall out," she says to Ryan.

He helps me up into the back to sit on the suitcases. Denise climbs in and sits next to me. Our cousins, Trevor and Dylan, climb in too. They want to come along for the ride.

In the front, my Auntie Claudia ask my mom if she has everything.

"Yes, the passport dem inna mi bag and I called Papa to remind him what time the flight's landing tonight," she answers.

"All right dear, Nadine and I will ketch a taxi and meet you all at the airport," says Aunt Claudia.

La camioneta ya está llena de maletas. "¿Puedo sentarme atrás con Ryan y Denise?" le pregunto a Mamá.

"Que se siente en un lugar donde no se vaya a caer," le dice Mamá a Ryan.

El me ayuda a sentarme atrás, encima de las maletas. Denise sube y se sienta a mi lado. Mis otros primos Trevor y Dylan también se suben. Quieren venir al aeropuerto.

Al frente, tía Claudia le pregunta a Mamá si tiene todos los papeles.

"Sí, tengo los pasaportes en la cartera, y llamé a Papá para recordarle a qué hora aterriza el avión."

"Bueno, Nadine y yo tomamos un taxi y nos vemos en el aeropuerto," Dice tía Claudia.

The van starts and we are off. We turn the bend and I see my school at the top of the hill. *Goodbye, Three Mile Basic School,* I think to myself as the breeze picks up.

I reach out and Denise holds my hand. A tear rolls down my face and I quickly wipe it away. Ryan catches me, but he doesn't say anything.

A gang of Ryan's friends are standing at the side of the road yelling to us as the van drives by. "All right Ryan! See yuh when yuh come back," they yell. "Bring one of those pretty girls they have over there!"

La camioneta arranca y nos vamos. Doblamos la curva y puedo ver mi escuela en la colina.

Adiós Three Mile Basic School, pienso mientras siento la brisa.

Me acerco a Denise y ella agarra mi mano. Una lágrima se escapa, pero la limpio rápidamente. Ryan me ve, pero no dice nada.

Un grupo de amigos de Ryan están parados al lado de la carretera, gritando.

"¡Adiós, Ryan! Nos vemos cuando regreses! ¡Trae una de esas chicas bonitas que tienen por allá!"

When we reach the town square, Mommy tells the driver to stop so she can say goodbye to some of her friends.

I look at my favorite cook shop. The red, green, and gold door swings open and someone comes out with a carry-out dish and pineapple-cherry box drinks. I'm going to miss Ms. Mabel's food. She makes the best rice and peas, and her curry goat is always just the right amount.

Right next door is Rasta. He's fixing his ice cream box and waves as he sees me looking. He walks over and hands all three of us a cone with mango ice cream. My favorite!

"A likkle something sweet to make your journey less bitter. Tek care of yourself, Likkle Miss," he says.

Mommy gets back into the van and we're off. I hope Chicago has mango ice cream too.

Cuando llegamos a la plaza, Mamá le pide al chofer que pare para despedirse de sus amigos.

Aquí veo mi cook shop favorito. La puerta roja, verde y dorada se abre y pasa alguien con un plato y un jugo de piña-cereza. Extrañaré la comida de la Señora Mabel. Ella hace el mejor curry goat (Curry de Cabra) y arroz con gandules.

A lado del cook shop está Rasta. Él está arreglando su caja y me saluda. Él camina y nos da tres helados de mango. ¡Mi favorito!

"Algo dulce para hacer tu viaje menos agrio."

Mamá regresa y arrancamos de nuevo. ¡Espero que haya helado de mango en Chicago también!

We pass Dr. Thorn's office and the secondary school. Denise and Ryan turn their heads to get a good look.

We drive past the field where Dylan, Ryan, and Trevor play football.

Coming down the street, I see my friend Diane and her mom. "All right Diane," I yell out. They wave as the van drives past.

We drive past cars blasting their music and see people stuffed in buses on their way to market.

We watch quietly, taking it all in. Before long, I hear a rumbling over my head. I look up and there's an airplane not too high in the sky.

"Wish we could come with you," Dylan says to Denise.

"Wish you all were coming too," she answers.

Pasamos la oficina de Dr. Thorn y la escuela secundaria. Denise y Ryan giran sus cabezas para echarles un buen vistazo.

Pasamos por el campo donde Ryan, Dylan y Trevor juegan futbol.

Caminando al lado de la carretera, veo a mi amiga Diane y a su mama. "Adiós, Diane," grito. Ellas me saludan mientras pasa la camioneta.

Pasamos autos que tocan música a todo volumen. Pasamos autobuses llenos de gente que van para el mercado. Vemos todo, con melancolía. Escucho un ruido sobre mi cabeza. Miro hacia arriba y veo un avión en el aire que no va muy alto.

"Me gustaría ir con ustedes," dice Dylan.

Eso nos gustaría también," dice Denise.

We arrive at the airport and no one is bothering to hide their faces. Tears are slowly rolling down cheeks and noses are sniffling.

The van pulls into a spot and Mommy double checks her bag to make sure she has everything.

"Oh gosh, don't cry. Yuh all know we'll come back to visit," she reminds us.

Ryan lifts me out of the back of the van. Dylan and Trevor unload the suitcases.

A taxi pulls up alongside us and Nadine jumps out and hugs me. She helps me roll my suitcase to the door.

"Race yuh to the counter," yells Ryan as he and Trevor take off with Mommy's suitcases. Nadine and I take off running behind them. Hope my suitcase doesn't tip!

Llegamos al aeropuerto y nadie se preocupa por ocultar sus rostros. Lágrimas corren por las mejillas y las narices resoplan.

La camioneta para y mamá revisa su bolsa para asegurarse que tiene todo.

"Ay, no lloren. Saben que vamos regresar a visitar a la familia," ella nos consuela.

Ryan me ayuda a salir de la camioneta. Dylan y Trevor descargan las maletas.

Un taxi se acerca y Nadine corre para abrazarme. Ella me ayuda a agarrar mi maleta.

"¡Una carrera al mostrador! " grita Ryan, él y Trevor empiezan a correr con las maletas de Mamá. Nadine y yo corremos detrás de ellos. Espero que no se caiga mi maleta.

We get to the line and what a line it is! Mommy and Denise catch up with us and Aunt Claudia, Dylan, and Trevor are right behind them pulling the rest of our luggage. All around us, people are hugging and saying their goodbyes.

The lady at the counter is really nice. I get the middle seat and Denise has the window seat. We watch as our suitcases are weighed and sent behind the counter.

"You'll enter through the door at the end of the hall and wait at Gate 5B," the lady tells us. "Boarding time is in 50 minutes."

Llegamos a la línea y es larga. Mamá, Denise, y tia Claudia nos alcanzan. Dylan, y Trevor siguen llevando el resto del equipaje. A nuestro alrededor, los demás se están abrazando y diciendose adiós.

La señora del mostrador es muy amistosa. Yo tengo el asiento del medio y Denise el de la ventana. Vemos cuánto pesan nuestras maletas y las envían atrás del mostrador.

"Entren por la puerta al fin del pasillo y esperen en la puerta 5B," nos dice ella. Embarcan en 50 minutos.

"Amoya, Denise, yuh hungry? Come mek we buy two patty while we wait," says Mommy. We all head toward Patty Palace.

I take Nadine's hand and we walk into Patty Palace together. Nadine pulls a little package out of her purse and hands it to me.

"Now yuh have no excuse," she tells me. "Yuh can write about everyting you see and do and send it to me!" I grin and give her a big hug.

Chicago, here we come!

"¿Amoya, Denise, tienen hambre? Vamos a comprar dos empanadas mientras esperamos," dice Mama. Caminamos hacia Patty Palace.

Le agarro la mano a Nadine y entramos a Patty Palace juntas. Nadine saca un paquete de su bolsa y me lo da.

"No tienes ninguna excusa", me dice ella. "Puedes escribir acerca de todo lo que ves y todo lo que haces!" Sonrie y me da un abrazo grande.

¡Chicago, aquí vamos!

GLOSSARY

FRY DUMPLING- Flour, baking powder, salt, and water, kneaded together to form dough. The dough is formed by hand into small balls and fried over low heat until golden brown

FOREIGN- Used to reference going to the Americas or United Kingdom, going to a "foreign" place, leaving Jamaica

FOOTBALL- Soccer

HORLICKS- A malted powder, usually mixed with milk or condensed milk and water. Can be served hot, as a tea, or cold

MEK- Let

MI- My

PATTIES- Seasoned beef stuffed inside a flaky crust; a beef turnover—similar to a Hot Pocket or empanada

VERANDA- A covered wrap-around porch in the front of a house or building

YUH- You

RECIPE FOR JAMAICAN FRIED DUMPLINGS

4 CUPS SELF-RISING FLOUR

1 TEASPOON SALT

1/2 CUP COLD WATER

1 CUP VEGETABLE OIL FOR FRYING

DIRECTIONS

1. In a large bowl, mix together the flour and salt. Mix in water, one tablespoon at a time, and knead until the mixture is a firm consistency. For a fluffier dumpling, let the dough sit covered for about 25 minutes.

2. Heat the oil in a large frying pan over medium heat until hot. Break off pieces of the dough and roll into a ball, flattening the top and bottom. Place the pieces into the frying pan, leaving a little space between each dumpling. Fry on each side until golden brown, approximately 3 minutes per side. Remove from the pan and drain on paper towels before serving.

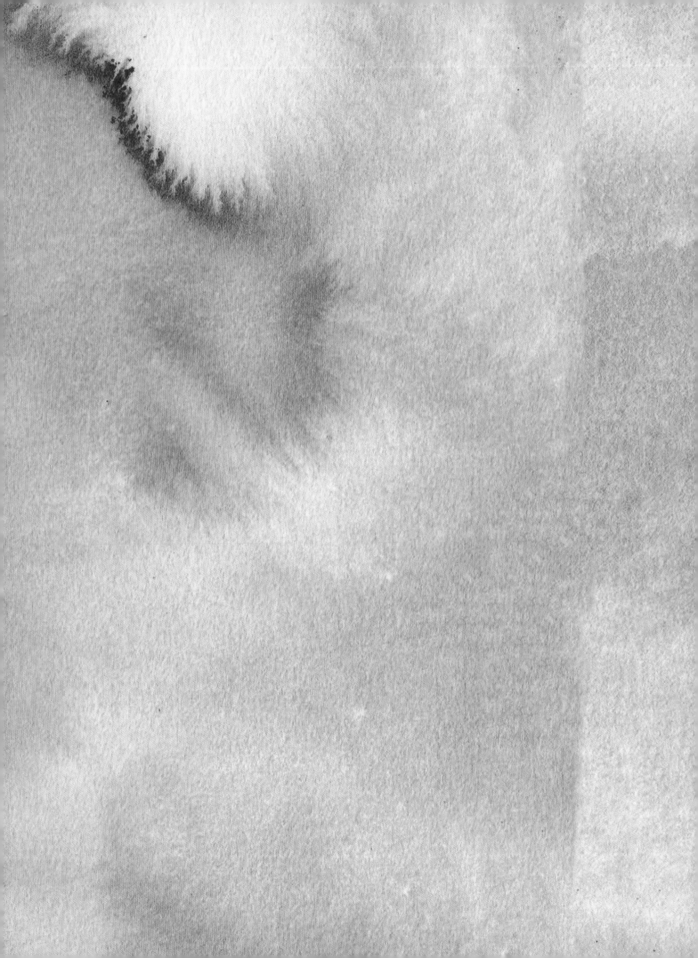

ABOUT THE AUTHOR

Graduating with a master's in Bilingual Education, Dahlia currently teaches third grade in Evanston, Illinois. Her family emigrated from Jamaica in 1987, and she was able to visit Jamaica for vacations every year. Reading has always been a very important part of her life, as well as a way for her to experience other cultures. She decided to write to share her experience of leaving her homeland and living in a culture very different from her own. This is her first book.

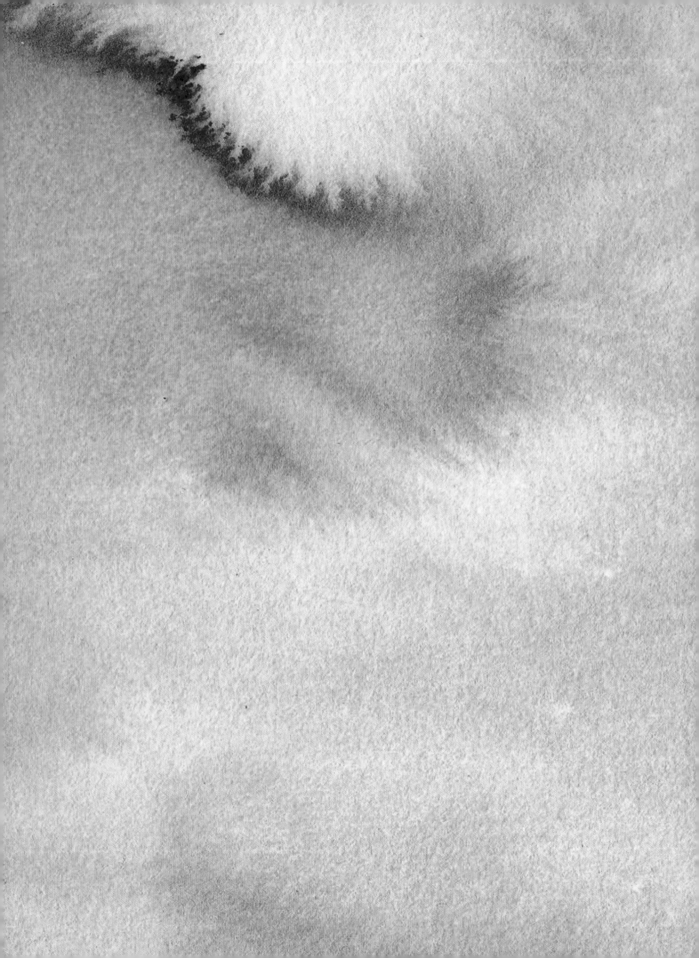